Geronimo Stilton
ENGLISH!

24 AT THE AIRPORT 在機場裏

U0106164

新雅文化事業有限公司
www.sunya.com.hk

Geronimo Stilton English
AT THE AIRPORT 在機場裏

作　　　者：Geronimo Stilton 謝利連摩・史提頓
譯　　　者：申倩
責任編輯：王燕參
封面繪圖：Giuseppe Facciotto
插圖繪畫：Claudio Cernuschi, Andrea Denegri, Daria Cerchi
內文設計：Angela Ficarelli, Raffaella Picozzi
出　　　版：新雅文化事業有限公司
　　　　　　香港英皇道499號北角工業大廈18樓
　　　　　　電話：（852）2138 7998
　　　　　　傳真：（852）2597 4003
　　　　　　網址：http://www.sunya.com.hk
　　　　　　電郵：marketing@sunya.com.hk
發　　　行：香港聯合書刊物流有限公司
　　　　　　香港新界大埔汀麗路36號中華商務印刷大廈3字樓
　　　　　　電話：（852）2150 2100　傳真：（852）2407 3062
　　　　　　電郵：info@suplogistics.com.hk
印　　　刷：C & C Offset Printing Co.,Ltd
　　　　　　香港新界大埔汀麗路36號
版　　　次：二〇一二年七月初版
　　　　　　10 9 8 7 6 5 4 3 2 1

版權所有・不准翻印
中文繁體字版權由 Atlantyca S.p.A. 授予
Original title: ALL'AEROPORTO
Based upon an original idea by Elisabetta Dami
www.geronimostilton.com

Geronimo Stilton names, characters and related indicia are copyright, trademark and exclusive license of Atlantyca S.p.A. All Rights Reseved.
The moral right of the author has been asserted.

Stilton is the name of a famous English cheese. It is a registered trademark of the Stilton Cheese Makers' Association.
For more information go to www.stiltoncheese.com

No part of this book may be stored, reproduced or transmitted in any form or by any means, electronic or mechanical, including photocopying, recording, or by any information storage and retrieval system, without written permission from the copyright holder. For information address Atlantyca S.p.A., via Leopardi 8 - 20123 Milan, Italy - foreignrights@atlantyca.it - www.atlantyca.com

ISBN: 978-962-08-5554-2
© 2008 Edizioni Piemme S.p.A., Via Tiziano 32 - 20145 Milano - Italia
International Rights © 2007 Atlantyca S.p.A. - via Leopardi, 8, Milano - Italy
© 2012 for this Work in Traditional Chinese language, Sun Ya Publications (HK) Ltd.
18/F, North Point Industrial Building, 499 King's Road, Hong Kong.
Published and printed in Hong Kong

CONTENTS
目錄

BENJAMIN'S CLASSMATES

班哲文的老師和同學們

Maestra Topitilla
托比蒂拉·德·托比莉斯

Rarin
拉琳

Diego
迪哥

Rupa
露芭

Tui
杜爾

David
大衛

Sakura
櫻花

Mohamed
穆哈麥德

Tian Kai
田凱

Oliver
奧利佛

Milenko
米蘭哥

Trippo
特里普

Carmen
卡敏

Atina
阿提娜

Esmeralda
愛絲梅拉達

Pandora
潘朵拉

Takeshi
北野

Kuti
菊花

Benjamin
班哲文

Hsing
阿星

Laura
羅拉

Kiku
奇哥

Antonia
安東妮婭

Liza
麗莎

GERONIMO AND HIS FRIENDS
謝利連摩和他的家鼠朋友們

謝利連摩・史提頓 Geronimo Stilton
一個古怪的傢伙，簡直可以說是一隻笨拙的文化鼠。他是《鼠民公報》的總裁，正花盡心思改變報紙業的歷史。

菲・史提頓 Tea Stilton
謝利連摩的妹妹，她是《鼠民公報》的特派記者，同時也是一個運動愛好者。

班哲文・史提頓 Benjamin Stilton
謝利連摩的小侄兒，常被叔叔稱作「我的小乳酪」，是一隻感情豐富的小老鼠。

潘朵拉・華之鼠 Pandora Woz
柏蒂・活力鼠的姨甥女、班哲文最好的朋友，是一隻活潑開朗的小老鼠。

柏蒂・活力鼠 Patty Spring
美麗迷人的電視新聞工作者，致力於她熱愛的電視事業。

賴皮 Trappola
謝利連摩的表弟，非常喜歡食物，風趣幽默，是一隻饞嘴、愛開玩笑的老鼠，善於將歡樂傳遞給每一隻鼠。

麗萍姑媽 Zia Lippa
謝利連摩的姑媽，對鼠十分友善，又和藹可親，只想將最好的給身邊的鼠。

艾拿 Iena
謝利連摩的好朋友，充滿活力，熱愛各項運動，他希望能把對運動的熱誠傳給謝利連摩。

史奎克・愛管閒事鼠 Ficcanaso Squitt
謝利連摩的好朋友，是一個非常有頭腦的私家偵探，總是穿着一件黃色的乾濕樓。

WHY ARE YOU SO QUIET?
你為什麼這樣安靜？

　　親愛的小朋友，我這幾天待在妙鼠城覺得很孤單……嗯，是這樣的，我的小侄兒班哲文和他的好朋友潘朵拉跟着我妹妹菲去了鯨魚島的鼠津城！雖然這兩個小傢伙總是會給我帶來很多麻煩，但是他們又同時給我帶來很多歡樂……我真的很掛念他們，於是我問柏蒂能不能陪我一起去找他們，我很久沒有去過鯨魚島的鼠津城了！

We miss you a lot.
我們很掛念你。

The kids' idea is great!
孩子們的主意真不錯！

The kids' idea is great! Why don't you ask Patty Spring to come with you?

Why not? I think it would be great fun!

跟我謝利連摩·史提頓一起學英文，就像玩遊戲一樣簡單好玩！

你可以一邊看着圖畫一邊讀。
以下有幾個標誌，你要特別留意：

當看到 🔘 標誌時，你可以聽CD，一邊聽，一邊跟着朗讀，還可以跟着一起唱歌。

當看到 ✪ 標誌時，你可以和朋友們一起玩遊戲，或者嘗試回答問題。題目很簡單，它們對鞏固你所學過的內容很有幫助。

當看到 ❗ 標誌時，你要注意看一下格子裏的生字，反覆唸幾遍，掌握發音。

最後，不要忘記完成小測驗和練習冊裏的問題！看看你有多聰明吧。

祝大家學得開開心心！

謝利連摩·史提頓

TWO TICKETS FOR TOPFORD
兩張去鼠津城的機票

我打電話給柏蒂邀請她一起去鯨魚島的鼠津城。柏蒂很開心地一口答應了，因為她也迫不及待想擁抱一下她的姨甥女潘朵拉。

1  *Hello?*

2  *Hi Geronimo! I've just spoken to the kids on the phone.*

Well, I'd like to.

4  *Really? They've just written me an e-mail. Why don't we join them?*

Then it's decided! I'll book two tickets!

5

When are we leaving?

6

See you soon, bye!

9

Good, I'm glad.

8

Next Friday.

7

8

我以一千塊莫澤雷勒乳酪發誓，我實在太想去鼠津城了，我甚至願意坐飛機去，要知道我可是很怕坐飛機的！我還馬上打電話給旅行社預訂我和柏蒂的機票呢。

I would like two plane tickets.

Where would you like to go, sir?

To Topford, on Whale Island!

Very well, sir. When would you like to leave?

Next week... if possible on Friday!

Ok, You can come and pick up your tickets tomorrow!

⭐ 試着用英語說出以下句子：

1. 你要去哪裏？

2. 你什麼時候出發？

答案：*1. Where would you like to go?*
2. When would you like to leave?

9

AT THE AIRPORT　在機場裏

我和柏蒂約好在機場碰面。我總是提前到達，不過柏蒂也很準時……我們可不想錯過航班！

Hostess: Please, place your baggage on the conveyor belt.
Geronimo: May I bring this bag as hand luggage?

Hostess: I'll check that it doesn't exceed the allowed measurements. Ok, you can take it with you. Here's your boarding pass: please go to Gate 3 in half an hour. Have a good flight!
Patty: Thank you, goodbye!

我和柏蒂在候機室聊天，這時廣播通知，我們的航班可以登機了！
我們馬上往登機閘口走去。

A SONG FOR YOU! Track 1

Hurry Up!

We have to catch a plane today!
Hurry up, it's already
on the runway.
It's fun to take the plane,

in a moment you can
go to Spain,
you are in the middle
of the clouds
that seem like whipped cream!

EXCUSE ME, WHERE IS MY SEAT?
請問我的座位在哪裏？

從候機室的大玻璃幕牆可以看到機場跑道，飛機停在上面等待起飛的指令。

landing

take-off

runway

tail

transfer bus

control tower

wing

passenger steps

airplane

hostess

steward

co-pilot

queue

pilot

flight attendants

我和柏蒂終於登上了飛機。為了可以更快找到座位，我請一位空中小姐幫忙。

FLYING IS FUN! 飛行真好玩！

坐上飛機後，我開始擔心起來，因為我有畏高症，而且我還擔心剛才在候機室裏吃的乳酪朱古力豆會不消化！柏蒂告訴我不要想太多，要注意聆聽機艙服務員的講解。

Above you there's an oxygen mask.

Under your seat there is a life jacket.

In case of an emergency landing on water, open the side exits manually.

Switch off your mobile phones and stow your tray table.

It's not dangerous. Come on, Geronimo, flying is fun!

Bring your seat to an upright position.

飛機飛行了一段時間後，空中小姐給乘客們提供小食。柏蒂愉快地接受了，但我因為胃痛，只要了一杯水。

I'd rather have… /
I would rather have…
我寧願要……

first class　頭等艙
business class　商務艙
economy class　經濟艙

A PERFECT LANDING
完美的降落

　　飛機終於降落了！我感覺好多了。我和柏蒂提取行李後，一走出機場，就見到菲和孩子們正在出口等我們，真是一個大驚喜啊！

 試着用英語說出：「我的安全帶在哪裏？」

答案：*Where's my seat belt?*

over there
在那裏

straight to the college
直接往大學去

TOPFORD COLLEGE
鼠津大學

菲獲邀請到她畢業的鼠津大學任教一個新聞系課程，她很開心可藉此機會與她的老朋友們見面，連班哲文和潘朵拉也很開心能認識到這些熱情的新朋友呢！

我以一千塊莫澤雷勒乳酪發誓，從菲的飛機上俯瞰鯨魚島真是美麗極了！這真是一個無法忘記的經歷……但對我來說，畏高症帶來的恐懼恐怕更難以忘記！

A SONG FOR YOU! Track 2

The Plane Flies in the Sky

Ladies and gentlemen,
the captain is speaking
you are kindly requested
to sit down and
fasten your seat belts...
I wish everyone a pleasant flight!

The plane flies in the sky
over the mountains, over the sea,
over the clouds.
The plane flies in the sky!
Ladies and gentlemen
we have now reached our destination
we hope you had a pleasant flight!

〈有備用乳酪嗎？〉

菲：我們終於來到機場了！

謝利連摩：我很開心我今天不用坐飛機。我害怕飛行。

艾拿：你說得對！我們來這裏是為了
接一個尊貴的乘客。

賴皮：在那裏！在那裏！我見到了……
謝利連摩：啊啊啊！

賴皮：來吧，謝利連摩！我知道你非常興
奮，但要冷靜啊！
謝利連摩：你把我嚇壞了！

班哲文：那裏！看！
謝利連摩：哦……太奇妙了！

謝利連摩：這是從英國直接運來的一整塊史提頓乳酪。妙極了！

旅客：喂，你！把我的車輪還給我！

謝利連摩：你說什麼？
旅客：那是我貨車的後備車輪呀！

艾拿：但……這真是乳酪！看！
旅客：我看不見！因為我的眼鏡在飛機上丟失了！

艾拿：你何不用口嘗嘗看？
旅客：你叫我吃車輪？

艾拿：相信我吧，嘗嘗看！
謝利連摩：但是……我的乳酪！
艾拿：我們犧牲一小口，總比失掉一整塊好！

旅客：哎……但……

旅客：他們把一個用乳酪製成的車輪賣給我！

The End

賴皮：現在……回家去！謝利連摩，把乳酪放在車尾箱吧！
菲：對，但不要把它和後備車輪混淆了！

TEST 小測驗

⭐ 1. 用英語説出下面的詞彙。

(a) 座位　　**(b)** 行李　　**(c)** 登機證　　**(d)** 機艙服務員　　**(e)** 機師

⭐ 2. 把下面的英文詞彙重新排列好，組成一個意思完整的句子。

| I | | like | | tickets | | two | | would |

⭐ 3. 下面的句子用英語該怎麼説？把正確的英文句子圈起來。

(a) 我們什麼時候出發？
　　A. When are we going?
　　B. When are we leaving?

(b) 下星期……如果可行的話，就星期天吧。
　　A. Next week... if possible on Sunday!
　　B. Next week... if possible on Friday!

⭐ 4. 空中小姐正在説什麼？用中文説出句子的意思。

Passengers are kindly requested to sit down and fasten their seat belts.

⭐ 5. 用英語説出下面的句子。

(a) 我剛剛和孩子們通了電話。
　　I've just spoken to ... ...

(b) 我會預訂兩張機票。
　　I'll ... ...

DICTIONARY 詞典

A

airplane 飛機

airport 機場

aisle 通道

allowed 准許

arrivals 到達

astronomical 天文的

at last 最後

B

baggage 行李

biscuits 餅乾

boarding pass 登機證

book 預訂

boot 車尾箱

business class 商務艙

C

calm down 冷靜下來

captain 機長

check 檢查

cheese 乳酪

clouds 雲

coffee 咖啡

college 大學

control tower 控制塔

conveyor belt 輸送帶

co-pilot 副機師

D

dangerous 危險

decided 決定

25

departure lounge　候機室

departures　離境

destination　目的地

fly　飛

G

gate　閘口

get ready　準備好

glasses　眼鏡

E

economy class　經濟艙

emergency exit　緊急出口

exceed　超過

excited　興奮

exits　出口

F

fasten　扣緊

first class　頭等艙

flight　飛行 / 航班

flight attendant　機艙服務員

H

hand luggage　手提行李

headphones　耳機

hostess　空中小姐

hurry　趕緊

I

inconvenience　不便

island　島

L

landing　降落

life jacket　救生衣

lost　丟失

M

miss　掛念

mobile phones　手提電話

mountain　山

N

nervous　緊張

O

observatory　氣象台

oxygen mask　氧氣面罩

P

passenger steps　乘客登機梯

passengers　乘客

passports　護照

pilot　機師

plane　飛機

position　位置

Q

queue　排隊

quiet　安靜

R

rector　校長

row　行

runway　跑道

S

sacrificing 犧牲

sandwich 三文治
（普：三明治）

screen 屏幕

sea 海

seat belts 安全帶

seats 座位

second 秒

security check 安全檢查

sell 賣

sit down 坐下

sky 天空

Spain 西班牙

spare 備用的

steward 空中少爺

suitcase 手提箱

switch off 關掉

T

take-off 起飛

tea 茶

tomorrow 明天

transfer bus 接駁巴士

truck 貨車

trust 相信

U

under 下面

upright 垂直的

W

water 水

wheel 車輪

when 什麼時候

where 哪裏

why 為什麼

window 窗子

wing 機翼

wonderful 奇妙

worry 擔心

看在一千塊莫澤雷勒乳酪的份上，你學得開心嗎？很開心，對不對？好極了！跟你一起跳舞唱歌我也很開心！我等着你下次繼續跟班哲文和潘朵拉一起玩一起學英語呀。現在要說再見了，當然是用英語說啦！

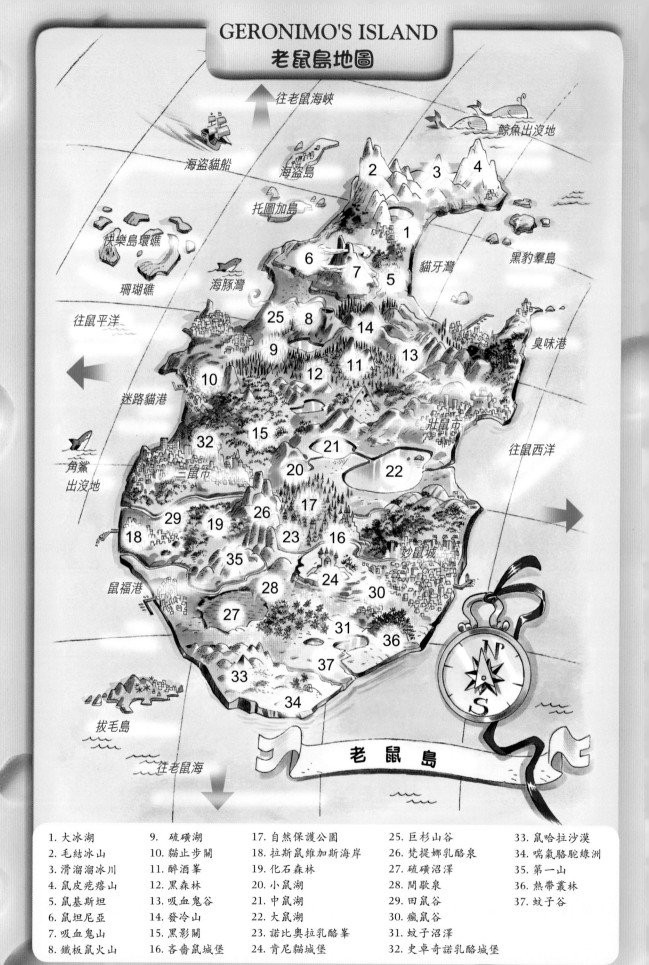

GERONIMO'S ISLAND
老鼠島地圖

往老鼠海峽

鯨魚出沒地

海盜貓船

海盜島

托圖加島

2　3　4

1

6　7　5　貓牙灣　黑豹羣島

快樂島環礁

珊瑚礁　海豚灣

25　8　14　臭味港

往鼠平洋

9　11　13

10　12　壯鼠市

角鯊
出沒地

15　32　21

20　22　往鼠西洋

三鼠市

迷路貓港

29　26　17

19　16

18　23

35

28　24　30

鼠福港

27　31　36

33　37

34

老　鼠　島

拔毛島

往老鼠海

妙鼠城

Geronimo Stilton

EXERCISE BOOK

練習冊

想知道自己對 AT THE AIRPORT 掌握了多少，
趕快打開後面的練習完成它吧！

ENGLISH!

24 AT THE AIRPORT　在機場裏

HELLO, UNCLE G!
你好，謝利連摩叔叔！

⭐ 班哲文和潘朵拉寫了一封電郵給謝利連摩，但電郵中有一些字不見了，從下面選出適當的字詞填在橫線上，把電郵補寫完整。

| miss you | don't you | having a lot of fun |

Hello, Uncle G! We are

_____ !

Why_____

come and visit us?

We_____a lot.

Kisses,

Pandora and Benjamin

A WEEK LATER...
一星期後……

⭐ 謝利連摩和柏蒂來到機場，準備出發去找班哲文和潘朵拉。想知道他們跟航空公司的職員在說什麼？從下面選出適當的字詞填在橫線上，就知道了。

> flight   thanks   conveyor belt   baggage
> hand luggage   goodbye   everything

1. Hello, Geronimo, _____ all right?

2. Yes, _____ ! Let's go and do our check in.

3. Hello! Please, place your _____ on the _____ !

4. May I bring this bag as _____ ?

5. Ok, you can take it with you. Please, go to Gate 3! Have a good _____ !

6. Thank you, _____ !

DEPARTURE LOUNGE
候機室

⭐ 1. 謝利連摩和柏蒂在候機室裏看到了什麼？從下面選出適當的
字詞填在圖畫旁的空格裏。

seats   passengers   baggage   airplane

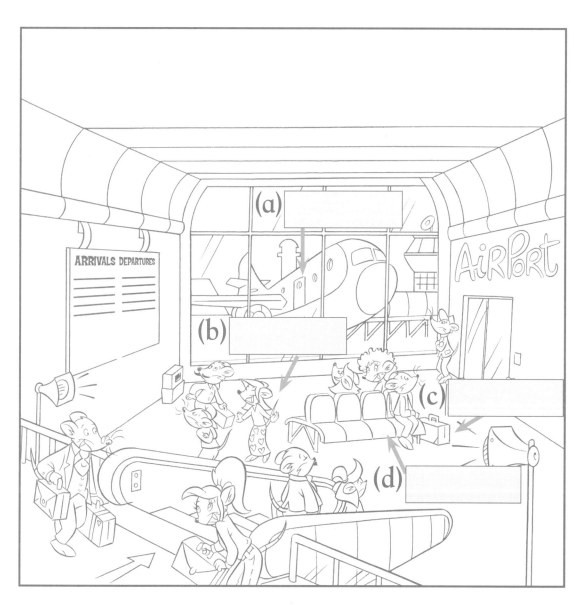

★2. 謝利連摩和柏蒂從候機室的大玻璃幕牆看出去，看到了跑道、接駁巴士……這些設施用英語該怎麼説呢？從下面選出適當的字詞填在圖畫旁的空格裏。

control tower   passenger steps   runway
wing   tail   transfer bus

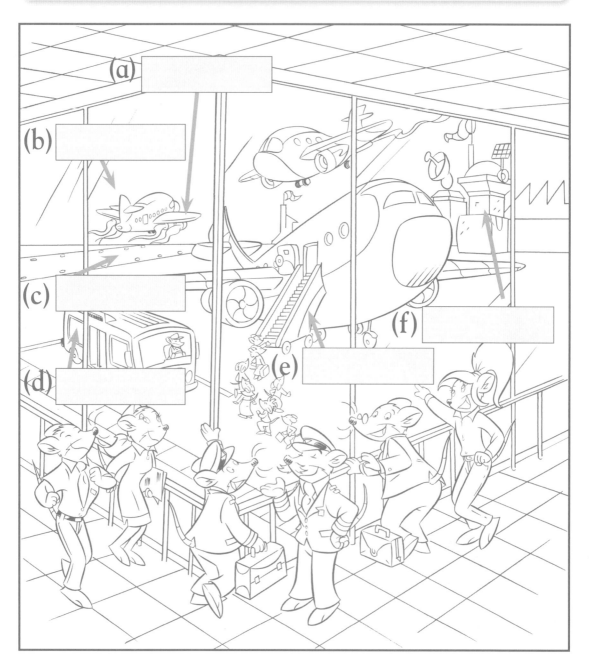

(a)

(b)

(c)

(d)

(e)

(f)

ON THE PLANE 在飛機上

⭐ 謝利連摩和柏蒂終於登上了飛機,想知道他們發生了什麼事?
把下面的字詞重新排列好,成為意思完整的句子,然後在橫線
上寫出來就知道了。

1. | my seat is | | tell me | | please | | where |
   | could you | | Excuse me | | ? | | , |

   _____

   _____

2. | boarding pass | | see | | May I | | your | | ? |

   _____

   _____

3. | flying | | afraid | | I'm | | of | | . |

   _____

   _____

4. | Don't | | everything | | worry | | all right |
   | will | | be | | , | | ! |

   _____

   _____

FLYING IS FUN!
飛行真好玩！

⭐ 空中小姐正在向乘客們講解在飛機上要注意的事項。從下面選出適當的字詞填在橫線上，完成空中小姐的話。

life jacket   mobile phones
side exits   oxygen mask

1. Under your seat there is a _____ _____.

2. Above you there is an _____ _____.

4. Switch off your _____ _____.

3. In case of emergency landing on water, open the _____ manually.

DURING THE FLIGHT
飛行途中

⭐ 飛機起飛了！謝利連摩、柏蒂和其他乘客們都安坐在座位上。
根據圖畫，從下面選出適當的字詞填在圖畫旁的空格裏。

> seat belt   window   headphones
> emergency exit   seat

ANSWERS 答案

TEST 小測驗

1. (a) seat   (b) baggage   (c) boarding pass   (d) flight attendant   (e) pilot

2. I would like two tickets.

3. (a) B. When are we leaving?   (b) A. Next week... if possible on Sunday!

4. 請乘客們坐好並繫上安全帶。

5. (a) I've just spoken to <u>the kids on the phone</u>.

    (b) I'll <u>book two tickets</u>.

EXERCISE BOOK 練習冊

P.1

Hello, Uncle G!

We are <u>having a lot of fun</u>!

Why <u>don't you</u> come and visit us?

We <u>miss you</u> a lot.

    Kisses,

    Pandora and Benjamin

P.2

1. everything   2. thanks   3. baggage, conveyor belt

4. hand luggage   5. flight   6. goodbye

P.3-4

1. (a) airplane   (b) passengers   (c) baggage   (d) seats

2. (a) wing   (b) tail   (c) runway   (d) transfer bus   (e) passenger steps   (f) control tower

P.5

1. Excuse me, could you please tell me where my seat is?   2. May I see your boarding pass?

3. I'm afraid of flying.   4. Don't worry, everything will be all right!

P.6

1. life jacket   2. oxygen mask   3. side exits   4. mobile phones

P.7

1. emergency exit   2. window   3. seat belt   4. headphones   5. seat